# The Rescue Princesses
## The Lost Gold

Princess Isabella frowned. What were the men doing? She hurried towards the sound, looking for any glimpse of movement. At last she saw something through the trees. Creeping forward, she hid behind a tree trunk, her heart beating faster and faster . . .

Have you read?

The Secret Promise

The Wishing Pearl

The Moonlit Mystery

The Stolen Crystals

The Snow Jewel

Look out for:

The Shimmering Stone

The Silver Locket

The Ice Diamond

# The Rescue Princesses
## The Lost Gold

**Paula Harrison**

nosy crow

# For Leni and Hester

First published in the UK in 2013 by Nosy Crow Ltd
The Crow's Nest, 10a Lant Street
London, SE1 1QR, UK

Nosy Crow and associated logos are trademarks and/or registered
trademarks of Nosy Crow Ltd

Text © Paula Harrison, 2013
Cover illustration © Sharon Tancredi, 2013
Interior illustrations © Artful Doodlers, 2013

5 7 9 10 8 6 4

A CIP catalogue record for this book is available from the British Library

Printed and bound in the UK by Clays Ltd, St Ives Plc

Papers used by Nosy Crow are made from wood grown in
sustainable forests.

ISBN: 978 0 85763 164 0

www.nosycrow.com

Chapter One

# The Blue Butterfly

Princess Isabella crept through the rainforest with a small monkey riding on her shoulder. Parrots squawked to each other in the treetops and water drops from the last rain shower glinted on the broad leaves.

Isabella's curly brown hair was loosely tied up with a ribbon and her dark eyes were determined. The butterfly that she was following had landed on a leaf and was flexing its beautiful wings. She held her breath and lifted up her camera slowly. It looked so perfect. The shiny wings were sky-blue with velvety black edges. She'd been trying to take a photo of a Blue Morpho butterfly for weeks and this was her chance!

"Stay really still, Petro," she whispered to the monkey. "This will make a great picture!"

She peered through the viewfinder, holding her finger just above the button. The butterfly looked quite small. If only she could get a little closer. She took a tiny step towards it, but her foot caught on a tree root and she stumbled. She grabbed at a branch to save herself but it snapped. Petro leapt off her shoulder, chattering crossly, and Isabella landed on the ground on her hands and knees.

Disturbed by the noise, the blue butterfly flew away into the treetops, its wings shimmering in the dappled sunlight.

"Oh, no!" Isabella watched it go before searching the ground for the camera she'd dropped. She found it and stood up, brushing the earth from her cherry-red dress. Petro ran along a branch, still chattering.

"I'm sorry, Petro!" Isabella checked the camera for scratches. "I thought I was getting better. I've been practising ninja moves every day, but it's no good!" She sighed heavily. "I still walk into things and trip over just as much as before."

Petro leapt gracefully down to her shoulder and nuzzled her ear. His soft tail curled lovingly round her neck.

"Thanks! You always cheer me up." Isabella smiled at the little brown monkey. She thought for a moment about her three new princess friends and how they had all promised to work on their ninja moves and other rescue skills. Well, she would just have to keep on practising!

She had met Princesses Lottie, Amina and Rosalind a few weeks ago at a royal dance festival. They'd decided to call themselves the Rescue Princesses and help any animals in danger, just like Lottie's older sister and her friends used to do.

They'd had an amazing adventure at the festival, saving some horses and a beautiful foal from being stolen. They had all become good friends, too. Now that Isabella was back home in the Kingdom of Belatina, she missed the other princesses a lot.

She smiled at Petro. "Maybe another butterfly will come past before we have to go back for lunch."

She cast a look at the tall towers of the palace behind her and then stepped deeper into the rainforest. Petro leapt off her shoulder and swung from tree to tree behind her. They often took walks here together. Isabella had found Petro alone in the forest when he was only a baby, and she had taken him back home and cared for him, saving fruit from her meals to feed him. When he was older, she'd thought that he would want to live in the wild again but he had refused to go and they had been best friends ever since.

Isabella stopped to look at a toucan with a huge golden beak, perching on a branch above her. This would make a good photo. She rested one hand on the thick tree trunk while she reached for her camera.

Suddenly, she froze. A sharp banging shattered the peace of the forest and the tree trunk trembled under her fingers.

"What's that, Petro?" she said. "I

haven't heard that noise before."

Petro's quick eyes darted all around and he ran back and forth along his branch.

After a few moments the banging happened again. It was louder this time and was followed by a high-pitched grinding sound that made Isabella shudder. Petro leapt back on to her shoulder and put his hands over his ears.

"Poor Petro!" said Isabella, stroking his soft, furry head. "I know you hate loud noises, but we have to find out what it is."

She hurried towards the sound, searching for what it could be. At last she saw something through the trees. Creeping forward, she hid behind a tree trunk, her heart beating faster and faster. There were a group of men standing in the middle of a clearing.

Isabella frowned. What were they doing? She hardly ever saw people in this part of the forest and never so many at once. And where had the clearing come from? She was sure there had been thick forest here before.

One of the men began to use a metal saw to cut a tree. The grinding noise grew louder as the saw bit into the trunk. The tree started to sway and, very slowly, it toppled over and crashed to the ground.

Isabella gasped. That was what the sounds were. They were cutting down the trees! She noticed several more fallen trees stacked to one side. This was terrible! The trees provided shelter and food for so many rainforest creatures.

These men had to be stopped. Should she go and tell them what they were doing was wrong? Just then, a small brown shape sprang out of a nearby tree and scampered across the clearing. It was a wild forest monkey and it looked

very frightened. A bunch of yellow fruit
fell to the ground. Isabella knew why the
monkey had been up the tree. Those fruits
were their favourite food.

"Hey!" yelled one of the men. "Get out
of here!" And he ran towards the monkey,
chasing it away.

Petro gave a squeak of fright and his
little hands dug into Isabella's shoulders.
Isabella felt so cross with the man she
thought she might burst.

"Don't worry, Petro," she whispered.
"We'll go back to the palace right now.
Once my mum and dad find out what's
going on, they'll tell these horrid men
to leave the forest alone." She took one
last look. One of the men was staring
curiously in their direction.

Isabella stayed completely still until
he'd turned away again. "Keep to the
shadows," she told Petro. "And let's run!"

## Chapter Two

# The Legend of the Lost Gold

Isabella raced back through the rainforest as quietly as she could. Petro moved from branch to branch, swinging through the treetops so he reached the palace grounds first. Hanging by his tail from the top of the silver gate, he waited for Isabella to catch up.

"I'm here, Petro," gasped Isabella, sprinting through the gateway and up the path. Her cherry-red dress swirled out behind her while the ribbon escaped from her curly brown hair and blew away in the breeze. Petro jumped down and galloped after her.

The palace of Belatina was made of gleaming white stone. At the front, a row of towering pillars reached up to a triangular shaped roof. Isabella ran past the long flowerbeds and up the broad stone steps to the front entrance. Ignoring the surprised looks of the guards at the front door, she dashed through the hallway and into the dining room to find her parents.

She skidded to a halt in front of them. Petro ran in behind her and jumped on to her shoulder.

"Mum! Dad!" she said breathlessly. "Something awful has happened! Some men are cutting down trees in the rainforest. Please come and stop them!"

Isabella stopped to draw breath and

realised that her parents didn't look half as alarmed as she'd expected.

"Slow down, Isabella, and tell us calmly what the matter is." Her mum, Queen Neva, poured herself a glass of pineapple juice. With her long brown hair and brown eyes, she looked just like her daughter.

Isabella took another breath. She noticed that her dad was staring at a piece of paper and hadn't even looked up. "Please, Dad! I need you to stop these men before they cut down too many trees."

"What's that?" Her dad finally looked at her. "Did you see some men working in the forest?"

Isabella nodded. She glanced at the piece of paper in her dad's hand. It was flecked with brown and crinkled at the edges.

"They're a group of treasure hunters, Isabella." King Victor rolled up the paper and fastened it with an elastic band. "You must keep out of their way. They have important work to do."

Isabella stared at him in astonishment. "But, Dad . . ." she began.

"You've heard of the legend of the lost gold, haven't you?" The king reached up to straighten his heavy crown. "It's such a famous story, after all."

"You know, dear. I used to tell you that story at bedtime when you were little," said Queen Neva.

"Oh! Yes, the lost gold. It's a good story," said Isabella. "But . . ."

"But it's NOT just a story!" said the king triumphantly. "The gold belonged to people that lived in our rainforest over a hundred years ago. So many people tried to steal it that they hid the treasure away.

Time went by and the gold was lost, but now we have a chance to find it again!"

Petro sprang lightly on to the table and began sorting through the oranges and mangoes while no one was paying attention.

The king held up the mysterious roll of paper, a dreamy look in his eyes. "This is the famous Silken Scroll, which has been kept safe in our palace for many years! It contains a secret code that tells where the gold is hidden. The treasure hunters have cracked the code. The legend says when the lost treasure is found, it will bring good luck and happiness to the whole kingdom."

"But what will we do with the treasure?" asked Isabella.

"Do with it?" The king frowned. "Well, keep it of course! In fact, the treasure hunters have offered me half of

everything they find!"

"But, Dad! What about the trees?" cried Isabella.

"Maybe they need to cut down a few trees so that they can dig in the right place." The king noticed Petro on the table. "Get that monkey off the table AT ONCE! That pet should not be in here at all. This is a royal dining room, not a zoo!"

Isabella leaned across, trying to catch hold of Petro, but her arm knocked over the glass jug and pineapple juice went splashing all over her mum.

"Isabella!" shrieked the queen, dabbing at her dress with a napkin.

Her screech made Petro jump in the air and he galloped across the table, knocking over the fruit bowl. Then he scampered out of the door.

"Sorry! I didn't mean to! I was just

trying to get hold of Petro." Isabella set the jug upright and started putting the fruit back into the bowl.

King Victor rose from his chair. "I shall put the Silken Scroll away in my desk before anything gets spilled on it."

"I'm really sorry about Petro getting on the table, Dad," said Isabella. "But please think about the trees! What will the monkeys do if these men cut down too many of their favourite fruit trees? It will be hard for them to find food."

The king looked down his long nose. "I know you mean to help, Isabella. But the monkeys do have plenty of other trees to choose from." He swept out of the room, taking the rolled-up scroll with him.

## Chapter Three

# The
# Jewels of
# Belatina

Isabella found Petro hiding behind a
large, brightly painted vase at the top
of the stairs. "It's all right, Petro. It was
really me that my dad was cross with."
She sighed. "I wish he understood about
the trees. It's not just the monkeys that
live in them. There are tree frogs and
lizards, parrots and toucans, and ever so
many other creatures."

Petro crept out from behind the vase
and nuzzled her hand before springing

up on to her shoulder.

"Isabella?" called Queen Neva. "Can you come here for a moment?"

Isabella found her mum sitting in front of the dressing-table mirror in her bedroom, fastening an earring into each ear.

"I know you're disappointed about the trees," said the queen. "But I don't suppose they'll cut down very many."

"The thing is that each tree gives food and shelter to animals," said Isabella. "I wish they didn't have to hunt for the gold."

"Finding olden-day treasure helps us to learn more about our country's past," said the queen, opening her green-velvet jewellery box. "All royal jewels have a story behind them. Soon I will teach you more about our crowns, necklaces and brooches, and where each one comes from." She took out a hair slide in the shape of a butterfly with wings made from gleaming sapphires. "This would look wonderful on you! Your hair does need tidying as you seem to have lost your hair ribbon. Would you like to try it on?"

Isabella tried to smile. "No, I . . . just don't really feel like it right now." She stared out of the window. In the distance she could see the palace wall and beyond that the forest.

Petro jumped lightly on to the dressing table and began sorting through the jewellery box. Then he picked up the butterfly hair slide, which looked huge in his little hands. He gazed at its sparkling blue surface.

"I know you're worried about the rainforest, but can't we do something to take your mind off it?" said Queen Neva.

Isabella opened her mouth to say that nothing would take her mind off the trees and the rainforest creatures she loved so much. But then a thought popped into her head. It was such an amazing idea that it made her eyes sparkle and her stomach flip over. She wasn't getting anywhere trying to protect the rainforest by herself, but maybe if she had some help . . . maybe then it would be easier.

"Mum?" she said carefully. "I met some other princesses when we went to the dance festival in the Kingdom of Peronia and I'd love to see them again. Could we have them to stay?"

Queen Neva scanned her face and then smiled. "What a good idea! That's just what you need – some other girls to do princess things with!"

Isabella tried very hard to keep a straight face. Her mum didn't know that she and her friends were more interested in rescuing animals than anything else!

"What are your friends' names?" said the queen. "I'll send them a royal invitation right away!"

"Thanks, Mum!" Isabella beamed. "There's Princess Lottie. She's from the Kingdom of Middingland. Then Princess Amina is from the Kingdom of Kamala by the eastern sea, and Princess Rosalind comes from Dalvia in the far north."

Her mum took a piece of paper out of a drawer and wrote down the names. "I will contact their parents today. Why don't you go and tell Cook that we might be having visitors to stay. We will certainly need to put on a special banquet to welcome them."

"I'll go straightaway!" Isabella hugged her mum. "Come on, Petro! Let's go and find Cook."

Petro managed to lift the blue butterfly hair slide right up and put it on top of his head. He chattered to his reflection in the mirror, as if he thought he looked very pretty.

Isabella giggled. "Oh, Petro! You can't keep that, you know! It belongs in the jewellery box."

She gently took the sapphire hair slide from his fingers and put it back. Then she lifted him on to her shoulder. Her heart raced as she went downstairs. She had to find somewhere secret to use her ring.

She looked around hurriedly and saw the small door underneath the stairs. Checking that no one was watching, she dashed inside, switched on the light and closed the door behind her.

She was in the royal broom cupboard. She only came in here if she was playing hide-and-seek with the maids. It was full of brushes and mops and ironing boards. Petro looked all around, his little face confused.

"No, we're not hiding, Petro," said Isabella. "I just wanted somewhere private to use my ring." She smiled as she looked at the yellow topaz ring on her finger.

One of the most exciting things about being a Rescue Princess was the magic rings Lottie had given them when they'd first met. The rings had come from her older sister, Emily, who had once been a Rescue Princess too. The girls had promised to call each other as soon as they found an animal that needed rescuing, and now Isabella had found a whole rainforest that was in danger!

Petro's quick eyes noticed what she was looking at. He darted down her arm and tapped on the yellow topaz with his little fingers.

"No, Petro!" laughed Isabella, covering the jewel with her other hand so that he couldn't touch it. "This ring lets me call the other princesses. You can't use it."

Carefully, she pressed the yellow topaz and held her breath. The jewel lit up brightly, sending a yellow glow across the walls of the cupboard.

Isabella raised her hand and spoke clearly into the jewel. "I have a message for the Rescue Princesses! This is Isabella. I need you to come and help the animals of the rainforest. I've persuaded my mum to invite you to stay."

She paused. She could hear faint noises through the jewel.

"Hello! This is Lottie!" came the reply. "That's great work, Isabella. See you soon!"

"This is Rosalind!" came a second voice.

"I'm glad we're doing another rescue at last, I was starting to wonder if anything would happen."

There was a gentle cough and a third voice came through. "Thanks for calling me, Isabella. This is Amina and I can't wait to see you!"

"Bye!" called Isabella. "See you all soon!" The yellow topaz jewel stopped glowing and she hugged Petro excitedly. She couldn't wait for the other princesses to get here!

## Chapter Four

# The Treasure Hunters

Isabella sneaked out of the royal broom cupboard with her cheeks flushed and her eyes sparkling. How long would it take for the other princesses to arrive? She hoped it wouldn't be too long! She went into the dining room to see if there was any lunch left out. Petro bounded on to the table and began picking bananas out of the fruit bowl.

Isabella was about to help herself to a sandwich from a silver dish when suddenly she heard an engine roaring and a large orange truck drove up to the front door. She went over to look out of the window. The truck stopped and a group of men climbed out. The king came hurrying down the front steps to meet them. Then they all went inside.

Isabella frowned deeply. She was sure they were the same men she'd seen cutting down the trees. So why were they here? She tiptoed down the hallway. Hearing voices inside her dad's study, she went closer and looked through a gap in the door.

She could see her dad sitting down at his desk with the scroll he'd shown her at lunchtime spread out in front of him. The visitors were sitting opposite.

"Thank you for seeing us, Your Majesty." The man who spoke had a square face and a black moustache.

"What is it, Mr Madelo?" said the king eagerly. "Have you found the gold?"

"No, we haven't found it yet, but we're very close now," replied the square-faced man. "And that's why we're here. We need to look at the Silken Scroll again, to work out the next part of the secret code."

"Yes, yes, of course!" said King Victor impatiently. "Here it is." He passed them the scroll and they all crowded round to look at it more closely.

"Hmm . . ." Mr Madelo looked at the crinkled, yellowy scroll. "This part of the code is difficult . . ." He traced a finger across the words on the paper and frowned.

"But can you work it out?" asked the king anxiously.

"Of course!" Mr Madelo smiled. "I have been breaking codes for many years. The gold will soon be mine . . . I mean, ours!"

"That's excellent!" cried the king.

Mr Madelo stood up and bowed. "We will return when we have more news for you."

Isabella stared at them through the crack in the door, her heart thumping. These men were about to start cutting down even more forest trees. She had to think of something fast!

She flung the study door open, fixing a wide smile to her face. "Good afternoon! Can I offer you some coffee and cake?"

The men looked startled. "Er . . . well . . ." began Mr Madelo. "That's very nice of you but—"

"It's our custom here in Belatina to offer guests something to eat," she said hopefully. "We wouldn't want you to go away hungry."

King Victor sighed. "I suppose that's true. Thank you for reminding me,

Isabella. Please tell Cook to send some refreshments in."

Isabella beamed and skipped along to the kitchens to find Josefina, their cook. "Josefina! Can we have some coffee and cake for my dad's visitors, please? And can I help you get it?"

Josefina, who was a short lady with a wide smile, put her apron on. "Of course you can, Princess Isabella! I baked a big chocolate cake this morning. You can get some plates and slice it up for me."

Isabella took the plates from the cupboard, sliced up the cake and set it all out on a tray. Then she carried the tray to her dad's study and Josefina followed her with the coffee. The cake looked delicious with its thick chocolatey icing but Isabella didn't take a slice. She wanted to save it all for the treasure hunters, because if they had second helpings it would take them even longer to go back to the rainforest. Then they would have even less time to chop down trees before night-time came!

The men ate the cake hungrily. Isabella's feeling of triumph faded as she watched them. They were eating too fast! They would be finished in a minute. The sun shone through the study window. It was still quite high in the sky, which meant there were hours to go till sunset.

Isabella raced back to the kitchen. "Josefina! I don't think these visitors come from our kingdom. Are there any local recipes that we can offer them?" She looked pleadingly at the cook.

"They can try my special nut and banana bread and after that they can have some mango ice cream," said Josefina. "Let me see what else I've got!"

Isabella took plates of the nut and

banana bread to the king's study.

"Our cook will be so pleased if you try this!" she said breathlessly. "I'll just fetch the mango ice cream and we have a special toffee sauce as well!"

After trying three more dishes, the men leaned back in their chairs, clutching their stomachs.

"Would you like some more ice cream?" said Isabella eagerly. "Or can I get you some lemonade?"

"I'm really very full," said Mr Madelo, wiping cake crumbs off his moustache.

"But please have something else—" began Isabella.

King Victor got up from his chair. "That's quite enough, Isabella. You've been very kind to our guests, but these men have a job to do." He led the treasure hunters to the front steps. "Let me know as soon as you find anything."

"We will, Your Majesty," said Mr Madelo.

Isabella watched sadly as the treasure hunters climbed back into their truck.

"Wait a minute!" said one of the men. "Where are the keys? I left them right here next to the steering wheel."

The men checked in their pockets and then searched the truck, but they couldn't find the keys anywhere.

"Perhaps you left them in my study?" suggested the king, hurrying back inside to look. But he came back empty-handed.

The men stood on the front steps of the palace, looking confused. "Surely someone wouldn't have taken them?" said Mr Madelo.

"Isabella, do you know where they are?" asked the king.

"No, I haven't seen them," said Isabella truthfully. She gazed around the palace garden, suddenly realising that she hadn't seen Petro since the treasure hunters arrived, and he usually spent most of the time by her side.

Then she spotted him and put her hand over her mouth to stop a giggle. Petro was dancing around on the smooth stone edge of the palace fountain. When he saw her watching, he jumped down from the fountain's edge and galloped away across the flowerbeds.

"We need our truck," said Mr Madelo. "Our equipment is much too heavy to carry."

"Fetch everyone in the palace," King Victor told the guards on the front door. "We must find the keys."

The next two hours were spent hunting all around the palace and the gardens for the truck keys. Everyone came to help except Josefina, who said she had far too much baking to do to spare the time. Everyone became hot and tired, and the sun dipped towards the tops of the trees.

Petro galloped over to Isabella as she searched another flowerbed. She was secretly delighted that the keys were lost; although she was sorry that it was making everyone else so cross.

"Petro, did you take the keys from the truck?" she whispered.

Petro leapt on to her shoulder and chattered into her ear.

"Hold on!" called the king, looking into the fountain. "I'm sure I can see something shiny in here." He rolled up the sleeve of his royal robe, plunged his hand into the water and lifted out the dripping keys. "At last! I've found them!"

"Thank you, Your Majesty!" Mr Madelo bowed as he took the keys. "It's too late to carry on our search for the treasure today because it will get dark soon. So we'll start again tomorrow morning."

The treasure hunters drove away and Isabella hid a smile as she and Petro walked back into the palace.

"Isabella!" her mum called. "Was it Petro who took the keys? He can be a little naughty sometimes!"

"I don't know," said Isabella truthfully. "I didn't see him take them."

As the queen turned away, Isabella whispered to Petro. "I bet it was you and I don't think it was naughty at all! I think it was very, very clever!"

# Chapter Five

# The Palace of Belatina

Isabella got up really early the next morning, hoping to find out when the other princesses would arrive. She was rushing downstairs to ask her mum about it when she heard the sound of a car drawing up outside, followed by girls' voices. Petro, who was swinging from the stair rail, pricked up his ears.

"Can they really be here already, Petro?" Isabella trembled with excitement as she yanked open the front door.

Three princesses were climbing the steps. Leading the way was Lottie with her green eyes and tight red curls, wearing a crimson dress. Behind them, their maids began unloading suitcases from the car.

"Hello! Did you miss us?" Lottie grinned and hugged Isabella.

"Yes, I did! I'm so happy to see you!" said Isabella. "How did you get here so quickly?"

"We all caught planes that flew overnight," explained Amina, smiling. Her long black hair hung over a turquoise dress that was fastened at one shoulder. "I've never flown during the night-time before. I slept most of the way."

"At least you didn't have to come from the Kingdom of Dalvia like I did," groaned Rosalind, trying to shake the creases from her blue dress. "It took such a long time to get here."

"Luckily, our planes landed at around the same time," Amina told Isabella. "And now we can't wait to help your rainforest animals!"

"Come and have some breakfast first," said Isabella. "You must be really hungry." She looked around for Petro as she led them inside. She really wanted the princesses to meet him, but she couldn't see him anywhere.

When they'd eaten breakfast, Queen Neva swept into the room. "Welcome to the Palace of Belatina, princesses!"

"Thank you so much for inviting us to stay," said Amina.

"Thank you," said Lottie and Rosalind, and they all curtsied.

"You're welcome, girls," said Queen Neva, with a smile. "Isabella will love having you here. You can do some lovely princess things together!" She looked doubtfully at Lottie's messy red curls. "Perhaps you would all like to unpack and tidy yourselves up a bit?"

"I'll help them take their suitcases upstairs," said Isabella hastily.

"Very well," said her mum.

Isabella showed her friends their rooms, which were on the top floor of the palace, next to her own. Then they met up in her bedroom to talk.

"You must tell us what the animal emergency is!" cried Lottie. "If I have to wait any longer to find out I'm going to burst!"

Isabella sat down under the yellow canopy of her huge four-poster bed and the others gathered round her. "It all started yesterday, when Petro and I heard a loud noise in the rainforest. When we went to look, we found out that there are men hunting for treasure and they're cutting down trees to make space to dig. They don't care how many forest creatures they hurt or that they've cut down some of the monkeys' favourite fruit trees." Her eyes filled with tears at the thought of it.

"Oh no! That's awful!" gasped Amina.

"How horrible!" Lottie's eyes flashed.

"Who's Petro?" said Rosalind.

"Oh! I forgot you hadn't seen him yet!" Isabella looked around, but there was still no sign of her monkey. "I really want you to meet him." She got up and opened her bedroom door. "Petro! Where are you?" she called down the corridor.

"Is he your brother?" asked Lottie.

"Or a cousin?" said Amina.

"No!" laughed Isabella. "Petro isn't a boy at all!"

There was a chattering sound near

the window. Then the curtains jiggled strangely.

Rosalind leapt off the bed, her eyes wide. "Isabella! I think there's something spooky near your window!"

Isabella rushed over and peeped round the edge of the yellow drapes. A little brown face with big eyes stared back at her. "Petro! Come out! It's not like you to be so shy."

Petro dangled from the curtains for a moment, then he leapt down to Isabella's shoulder. She stroked his head lovingly.

"Oh! He's a monkey!" cried Lottie, and the girls began to laugh.

"This is Petro. I found him all alone in the forest when he was a baby," explained Isabella. "So I brought him back here and looked after him. We've been great friends ever since."

"You're so lucky!" said Rosalind. "I have

two dogs, three cats and a hamster, but I haven't got a monkey." She gently rubbed Petro's furry ears. Amina and Lottie came over to stroke him too. Petro curled his tail round his toes and chattered a friendly greeting.

"See! There was nothing to be afraid of," Isabella said to Petro. "Monkeys aren't really supposed to be kept as pets," she told the princesses. "But Petro can go back into the rainforest whenever he wants. Usually we go together! I think of him as more of a friend than a pet."

"But what about all the other monkeys – the ones whose trees are being cut down," Lottie reminded them. "We should start planning how to help them."

"Won't your mum and dad tell the men to stop chopping down the trees?" Amina asked Isabella.

Isabella shook her head. "I've tried to

talk to my parents about it already."

"How about we scare the treasure hunters away!" suggested Rosalind excitedly. "We could sneak up on them using our ninja moves and then frighten them."

"There are quite a few of them, so I don't think they'll get scared that easily," said Isabella.

Rosalind pouted. "Well, I thought it was a good idea."

"What is it that they're searching for?" asked Amina.

"Some lost gold that was hidden in the forest long ago," sighed Isabella. "That's what they want. I just wish they didn't have to hurt the trees and animals to find it."

Amina looked thoughtful. "Why don't we find it first? Then they have no reason to carry on with what they're doing."

"It would certainly teach them a lesson," said Rosalind.

"How are we going to do that, though?" said Lottie.

"I know! My dad's got the Silken Scroll in his study," said Isabella. "It's like an ancient treasure guide that explains how to find the gold, and the clues are written in a secret code. If we can work out the code, it will tell us what to do!"

## Chapter Six

# Ninja Outfits

"Let's go downstairs right now and see if we can get a peek at the scroll!" said Isabella, her eyes shining.

"Just a minute!" said Lottie. "I brought something that might help with our adventures. I'll fetch it."

"I brought something too," said Rosalind. "It's in my suitcase." And both girls rushed from the room.

Isabella and Amina looked at each other. "Do you know what they're talking about?" asked Isabella.

Amina shook her head.

Rosalind returned first, carrying a blue bag made from a soft velvety material. "I've been thinking about the ninja moves that we used when we rescued those horses a few weeks ago," she said breathlessly. "I decided that we needed some ninja outfits that suited different places and I got my maid to help me make them."

"Wow, Rosalind!" said Isabella. "I can't believe you did all that!"

Rosalind looked pleased. "These are the ones I made for doing ninja moves in a forest." She pulled a collection of dark green T-shirts and leggings from the bag and held them up to show the others.

"You're really into using ninja moves, aren't you?" said Amina.

Rosalind nodded. "I've been practising

lots. I'd really like to find that lost book, the *Book of Ninja*, that has every single ninja move inside it." She stopped suddenly as the door swung open, but it was only Lottie returning with a large golden box.

"Those look great!" said Lottie, looking at Rosalind's ninja outfits. "We'll really be camouflaged among the trees wearing green."

Rosalind put the clothes down. "And what did you bring?" she asked curiously.

"Remember how I told you that my sister and her friends used to rescue animals, and how they shaped magic jewels to help them?" said Lottie. "Well, my sister gave me this box so that we could have a go at making them ourselves!"

She opened the golden box and showed them a collection of small silver tools.

Then she pulled out a hidden drawer underneath to reveal a heap of jewels in every shape, size and colour. Rubies, sapphires, emeralds and diamonds, all sparkled in the morning light.

"Amazing!" gasped Amina. "Your sister is really kind, Lottie."

Lottie shrugged. "She's OK sometimes, I suppose. There are some instructions about how to use the tools. I thought we could have a go later."

"That would be awesome!" Isabella shook back her curly brown hair, her eyes shining. "Let's put on the ninja clothes right now and then go downstairs to look at the treasure guide. After that we'll be ready to go straight out into the forest."

"Let's take a rucksack with us too," said Lottie sensibly. "We might need water and snacks later on."

Through the window came the distant

sound of banging and sawing.

"That's probably the treasure hunters. They're cutting down another tree already," said Isabella. "Let's hurry."

The princesses quickly changed into the green T-shirts and leggings, while Petro leapt around the room excitedly and dangled from the lampshade.

Lottie borrowed Isabella's rucksack and packed it with food, drink and some of the jewel-making tools. Then she put it on her back. When they were all ready, Rosalind opened the bedroom door a tiny crack. "There's no one out here," she whispered. "I think it's safe to go!"

"Now remember, Petro, don't give us away!" Isabella put a finger to her lips to show the little monkey that he should be quiet. Petro sprang on to her shoulder and obediently put his hand over his mouth.

Together, they sneaked along the
corridor to the top of the stairs and
looked down. The hallway was empty
and the palace seemed really quiet. So
Isabella led them down the stairs and
over to the door of her dad's study.

She listened for a moment. There was
no sound from inside, so she crept in and
hurried over to her dad's desk.

"Is the scroll there?" asked Rosalind.

"I can't see it," said Isabella. "But
maybe my dad's put it in one of the
drawers."

Lottie closed the door and put her ear
to it. "I'll stand here and listen in case
anyone comes along."

There were three drawers in the desk.
Isabella bent down to open the first one,
and accidentally knocked over the chair
behind her which fell to the floor with a
loud thump. "Sorry!" she said. "I didn't

mean to do that."

Rosalind sighed. "We'll have to hurry now. Someone might come to find out what the noise was."

"I'll be quick." Isabella flushed deeply and opened the first drawer, but it only had pens and pencils inside it. Amina looked in the second drawer, but that was full of blank paper. Then Isabella pulled open the last drawer and instantly recognised the scroll, which was rolled up and fastened with an elastic band.

"I've got it!" she grinned. Gently, she pulled off the band and unrolled the paper, which was yellow with age and crinkled at the edges.

"I can't wait to see the secret code!" said Rosalind.

The scroll was covered with writing and had a small picture in the middle. Isabella's heart sank. The paper was so

old that the words were hard to read. What if she couldn't even work out what the letters were?

Just then, Lottie waved her hand for them to be quiet. There was a noise in the corridor.

"Now where have those princesses gone?" said Queen Neva, her footsteps coming closer. "Have you seen them, Josefina?"

"No, I haven't, Your Majesty," came Josefina's reply.

"That's very strange, because the guards say they haven't gone outside and yet I can't find them in any of the rooms," Queen Neva went on. "I was just about to ask them if they wanted to learn the history of our royal crowns and tiaras. I wonder if there's anywhere I haven't looked."

The girls held their breath as the

queen's footsteps came even nearer.
Isabella stared at the door anxiously.
What would her mum say if she caught
them all in here, looking in the king's
desk and wearing strange green ninja
clothes?

Then, just as she expected her mum to
burst in, a faint chattering noise started.

"What's that?" Queen Neva's voice was
right outside the door. "Petro, what's
that shiny thing that you're holding?
Have you been into my room and taken
something from my jewellery box? Come
back at once!" Her footsteps sped up, but
grew fainter.

Lottie opened the door a tiny crack.
"Petro's saved us! The queen's followed
him upstairs."

Isabella carefully rolled up the Silken
Scroll and put the elastic band back on.
"Let's go quickly, before my mum

comes back!"

So they tiptoed down the hallway and out of the front door, then ran across the garden towards the rainforest.

## Chapter Seven

# The Silken Scroll

The princesses ran through the front gate, only slowing down once they reached the trees. A brown shape came bounding across the palace garden to join them.

Isabella called to the little monkey. "Petro! You were such a star, you stopped us being caught!"

"What is he holding?" said Lottie.

Petro swung over the palace gate and jumped down to the ground. Something blue and sparkly gleamed in his hand.

"Come here, Petro." Isabella knelt and beckoned him closer. He bounced over to her and she took a butterfly hair slide from his grasp. It was the one with the sapphire wings that he had been playing with the day before.

"Oh dear! You shouldn't have taken this," Isabella told him. "It's not yours."

"Who does it belong to?" said Rosalind.

"It's from my mum's jewellery box and it's very precious." Isabella held the butterfly-shaped hair slide out to show them. The sapphire jewels on its wings shone a beautiful deep blue. "We'll have to return it, but let's find the treasure first, there's no time to lose." She handed the hair slide to Lottie, who put it away safely in the rucksack on her shoulder.

The princesses ran on into the rainforest. Isabella led the way along the paths she knew so well. Lottie, Amina and Rosalind followed her, staring in amazement at the brightly coloured parrots and the toucans with their golden beaks.

"Wow!" said Lottie. "Look at that red frog; I've never seen one as bright as that before."

"And look! Aren't they lovely?" Rosalind pointed at a troop of small monkeys swinging through the trees at top speed. One was carrying a tiny baby on its back.

"They look as if something's scared them." Isabella bit her lip. "I bet they're running away from the treasure hunters with their axes and saws." She unrolled the scroll. "Horrible men! We *must* work out where the gold is before they do."

The girls crowded round the paper, which had rough edges and cracks running across it. The writing was squiggly and the ink was faded, but as they stared at it they began to make out what it said.

"Look! Here's the symbol for north, south, east and west," said Amina.

"And the picture in the middle shows us where the river is." Isabella pointed at a curved line running across the small picture. "The palace isn't on here, but I guess that's because this scroll was written before the palace was even built."

"Where's the hidden treasure, though?" said Rosalind.

Isabella squinted at the letters. They were long and curly, which made them quite hard to read, and splodges and cracks covered parts of some of the letters. "I live in the . . . forest." She read the first line haltingly. "Ooh, how funny! They made the dot on top of the letter 'I' into a monkey's face!"

"There's a monkey's face on every line,

look!" Lottie pointed to the little monkey faces. "It looks like they're above certain letters."

"What do the other lines say?" demanded Rosalind.

"Just a minute, some of the words are hard to see because the paper is so old."

Isabella took a deep breath and read:

I live in the forest
I am small and funny.
I swing high and low
Loving the shady trees
With their branches and leaves
And delicious fruit
What am I?

"It's a riddle," said Lottie. "I think it's describing an animal."

"I think so, too," agreed Amina. "An animal that's small and funny."

Petro leapt on to Isabella's shoulder, chattering loudly. Isabella laughed. "Petro knows what the animal is!"

"Of course!" said Lottie. "Small and funny – it's a monkey!"

"But how does that help us find the gold?" said Rosalind. "Does it mean that the monkeys know where the treasure is?"

"No, they can't! It was hidden too long ago," said Isabella, frowning.

The princesses all looked puzzled. "Let's carry on walking and look for clues," said Lottie, at last. "Maybe the picture will help us."

As they walked on, the sound of banging and sawing grew louder and they could hear the treasure hunters shouting to each other. The ground sloped down to a wide river with trees all the way along the banks.

There was more noise from the treasure hunters up ahead. Isabella put a finger to her lips and beckoned to the others. They hid behind a tree with a wide trunk and peered out. They could see the treasure hunters standing beside two fallen trees not far from the riverbank.

"There's no sign of the gold here," said one man. "Are you sure we're looking in the right place?"

"I've no idea!" replied Mr Madelo. "It must be around here somewhere."

"But you told the king you'd cracked the code on the scroll," said another man.

"Of course I've cracked it!" said Mr Madelo. "It's just a crummy old bit of paper with a silly riddle that means monkey. That doesn't help us at all.

We just have to keep on cutting down trees until we find something." He aimed a kick at one of the fallen trees.

"What a waste of two lovely trees," whispered Lottie.

"And how terrible for all the creatures that lived in them," said Amina.

Isabella's eyes flashed. "I'm sure there is a real clue somewhere on the Silken Scroll and we're going to find it! We *won't* let them destroy this beautiful forest!"

## Chapter Eight

# Monkey Island

Isabella stared at the Silken Scroll once more. "The riddle does mean monkey," she muttered. "But maybe the little faces mean something too."

"You mean the monkey faces?" said Amina. "Do you think they're above certain letters for a reason?"

"I think we should keep on walking and look out for clues in the forest," said Rosalind. "And I'm glad the treasure hunters haven't chopped down those trees. See all the monkeys living there?"

Rosalind pointed at a group of trees
on the other side of the river. They were
full of monkeys jumping from branch
to branch and chattering to each other.
Petro watched them closely, as if he was
ready to leap away and join them.

"That's actually a little island in the
middle of the river," Isabella told her.
"Lots of monkeys like living there. I
guess they feel safe." Her eyes suddenly
widened as she stared at the scroll in her
hand. "Hold on! The monkey face on the
first line is above the letter I. Then on line
two it's by an S, then an L, then A, N, D."

"So it's I, S, L, A, N, D," said Lottie
thoughtfully. "And the riddle means
monkey."

"It's Monkey Island!" they burst out
altogether. Then they had to duck down
to hide as the treasure hunters turned in

their direction.

"What was that sound?" said one man.

"Probably another silly parrot," said Mr Madelo. "Come on now, get back to work."

"The lost gold must be on Monkey Island," whispered Isabella, as soon as the men had turned away. "It must have been there all this time!"

"But how do we get across? Is there a bridge?" asked Rosalind.

Isabella shook her head. "Either we have to swing across like Petro or make a bridge ourselves."

"Let's swing," whispered Amina, but the others shook their heads.

"I'd rather use a bridge," said Lottie. "I'm sure I'd be much less likely to fall in."

"One of those fallen trees would make a good bridge. It's a shame they're too heavy for us to carry," said Rosalind.

"But we might be able to lift that big branch over there." Isabella pointed at a sturdy branch that had broken off one of the fallen trees. "Look, the men are going back to their truck. If we're quick we could get the branch right now. Then we could cross to the island without them ever seeing us."

The princesses sneaked forward, glad that they were camouflaged in their green ninja clothes. The treasure hunters were standing next to their truck not far away. From the clashes and clanks, it sounded as if they were unloading more tools.

Isabella raced to one end of the branch, while Lottie stood at the other end and Rosalind and Amina went in the middle.

"Ready, everyone?" whispered Isabella.

Together, they all heaved the branch upwards.

"It's heavy!" gasped Amina.

"Quickly, before they come back!" hissed Lottie.

Isabella looked at the treasure hunters, but luckily they were still busy by the truck. Her arms began to ache as she led the way down to the riverbank. Her foot caught on a tree root and she nearly lost her balance. Holding the branch tightly, she told herself to be careful. She couldn't ruin everything by tripping over.

"Let's go a bit further," muttered Lottie. "We need to be sure that those men can't see what we're doing."

They trudged along the bank until they found a place where the river was narrow and they were hidden from view by the trees.

"But how are we going to lay the branch across so that it makes a proper bridge?" asked Amina.

"It would be easier if one of us could swing across and catch it on the other side." Isabella smiled at Amina. "Do you think you could do that? You are better at gymnastics than the rest of us!"

"I'll try!" Amina said. She climbed a tree that stretched out over the water and managed to swing across to the opposite bank. Petro followed her, chattering excitedly.

"That was brilliant!" said Lottie. "Are you ready to catch the branch?"

Amina pushed back her long dark hair. "Yes, ready," she said.

Petro dangled from a tree by his tail, enjoying the whole adventure.

Together, Isabella, Lottie and Rosalind heaved the branch across the river. It was hard work and Isabella began to worry that the branch might fall in and sink below the water. At last they pushed it across. Amina caught hold of it on the other side and dragged it into place.

Isabella put one foot on the thick branch and it wobbled frantically. How would she ever manage to get across? She found it so hard to keep her balance.

"Just keep going and don't look down," advised Lottie.

Isabella held her breath as she tiptoed across, her arms stretched out on either side. Right in the middle the branch trembled again and she thought she was going to fall in. But she kept going until she was safely on the opposite bank.

"Well done!" whispered Amina, squeezing her hand.

Isabella grinned. "Thanks."

Petro dropped down on to her shoulder and nuzzled her ear.

One by one, Lottie and Rosalind crossed

the river. When they were all safely on the other side, Isabella unfurled the Silken Scroll again. A group of monkeys swung down from the treetops and stared curiously at the girls. Petro leapt from Isabella's shoulder into the branches to play with them.

"Look!" Isabella turned the scroll over. "There are two more lines of writing on the other side." Just then, the sound of banging and sawing started up again. "Oh! Those horrid men are cutting down another tree. We have to hurry!"

"Let me try," said Amina calmly. "I think the first line says: *Find the tallest tree.*"

"Well, that should be easy! Let's find it right now." Isabella led the way, crashing through some bushes and making a long-snouted animal run away in fright.

"What is that?" Rosalind stared

wide-eyed at the dark, pig-like creature.

"It's a tapir," said Isabella. "Don't worry, it won't hurt you."

"Wasn't the scroll written a long time ago?" said Lottie, frowning. "Maybe the tall tree they were talking about has fallen down since then."

"Some of the trees in this rainforest are hundreds of years old," said Isabella. "So it might still be here."

"How about that one!" cried Amina, pointing at a huge tree whose branches soared far above the others.

They rushed over and gazed up at its thick trunk.

Isabella's heart was racing. "What does the last bit of writing say?" she asked breathlessly.

"*Look in the heart of the tree and you will find the gold,*" Amina read slowly. "I don't really understand that part."

"*The heart of the tree,*" echoed Isabella. "I wonder where that is?" She walked all around the trunk, looking at every mark and crack in the wood.

"Everyone get behind the tree!" hissed Lottie. "There's a man looking across at this island."

They all hid behind the tree. The treasure hunter walked along the riverbank and noticed the branch they'd laid across the river as a bridge. He scratched his head.

"I hope he doesn't cross over," muttered Isabella, "because if he does we're in really big trouble!"

## Chapter Nine

# Rainforest Treasure

The princesses watched the man for several minutes as he looked at their bridge and stared across at the island. At last he wandered back towards the other men.

"That was close," muttered Lottie. "I don't think he saw us."

"But where are we supposed to look for this gold? Maybe we have to climb up the tree?" suggested Rosalind.

"The guide says: *the heart of the tree,*

and I think that really means the roots."
Isabella crouched down to look at the
base of the tree. The roots jutted out of
the ground and there were gaps between
them. She caught a glimpse of something
hidden in there.

"I can see something!" She reached
into the hollow between two roots and
dragged out an old leather bag with a
strap covered in red beads. A couple of
beads fell off it and rolled away. The bag
felt really heavy and something jingled
inside it.

"Let's see what's in there," said
Rosalind excitedly.

Isabella undid the fastenings and a
bright glow burst from the bag. She put
her hand in and took out a small golden
statue. "Look at this! It's beautiful!"

"That's amazing!" Amina reached in
and pulled out a handful of gold coins.

Lottie delved into the bag and took out a large golden mask in the shape of a monkey's head. "Wow! This treasure is awesome!"

"Let's take everything back to the palace," said Isabella. "Once we've shown this to my dad, he can tell the men to stop hunting for the treasure. Then all the trees and creatures will be safe again."

But as she stood up, a shout came from across the water. The treasure hunters were standing on the edge of the river and looking straight at them.

"Hey!" shouted one. "What are you girls doing with our gold?"

"They've seen us! What shall we do?" gasped Amina.

"We have to get across the river and back to the palace as fast as we can!" said Lottie.

Isabella tried to lift up the old leather bag, but she couldn't. "I can't move this, the gold is so heavy!"

"Let's all lift it together." Lottie's green eyes were determined.

So they all grabbed hold of the bag, but it still didn't move.

A yell came across the river. "Hey! Put that gold back or you'll be sorry!" It was Mr Madelo, his black moustache twitching. He turned to the other men. "Find a way to get over to that island and get the gold off them!"

The men ran along the riverbank towards the branch that the girls had used as a bridge.

"Rosalind! Amina!" hissed Isabella. "Try to get rid of the bridge we made. See if you can push it into the water."

Rosalind and Amina dashed away to the water's edge.

Startled by all the shouting, the monkeys in the treetops began calling loudly to each other.

"What shall we do?" Isabella asked Lottie. "Even without the branch bridge those men will find a way over here in the end and the gold's too heavy for us to move. Why should they get the treasure after all the bad things they've done?"

"Give up the gold, right now!" bellowed Mr Madelo. "Or we will cut down every single tree on that island."

Isabella's heart sank. The island's trees were home to so many monkeys. What if they got hurt?

Lottie's face turned as red as her curls. "We won't give up!" she said fiercely. "There must be a way to stop them!" She took off her rucksack and looked inside it.

"What about these jewel-crafting tools?" Isabella reached into the rucksack and pulled out a small chisel.

"But I didn't put any jewels in the rucksack and there are only gold things in that treasure bag," said Lottie.

"How about the butterfly hair slide that Petro took from my mum's room?" said Isabella, rummaging inside the rucksack to find it. "That's made from sapphires. Maybe we can use that."

There was a loud splash and a cheer from Amina and Rosalind as they managed to push the branch bridge into the water. The treasure hunters stood on the opposite bank, glaring angrily.

Lottie drew some scribbled instructions from the bottom of the rucksack. "This tells us how to make a jewel glow or how to make it heat up, but that won't help us."

Isabella put down the tools and picked

up a tiny pot. "What does this do?"

"It's some kind of polish," said Lottie. "I can't see how that would help us, either."

*Bang!* The ear-splitting noise made the girls jump. One of the treasure hunters was chopping down a tree right next to the river.

"We'll make our own bridge using this tree!" shouted Mr Madelo. "Then we're coming over there to get our treasure!"

Suddenly, Isabella noticed a baby monkey clinging on to the tree they were chopping down. "Stop!" she yelled to them. "There's a baby monkey right at the top of that tree. You'll hurt him if you carry on!"

But the men ignored her, their sharp axes cutting into the trunk. The tree wobbled and the tiny monkey swayed with it. His eyes were round with fear as

he held tight to his branch and looked
down at the treasure hunters below.

## Chapter Ten

# The Butterfly Hair Slide

"The poor thing!" said Isabella. "He must have been left behind when the other monkeys got scared and ran away."

"How can we help him?" cried Lottie. "We're so far away across the river."

"I don't know!" Isabella stared at the jewelled hair slide and the jewel-making tools strewn around her. Desperately, she pulled the lid off the pot of polish and looked at the silver cream inside.

She took some of the polish and

smeared it on to the sapphire wings of
the butterfly hair slide. It glittered for
a moment before disappearing. Then
suddenly, the hair slide began to feel
incredibly light. The sapphire wings
flapped gently and the whole hair slide
rose up into the air and hovered just
above her hand.

"That's amazing!" gasped Lottie. "Did
the polish make it do that?"

"Yes! All I did was put some on to the
jewels," said Isabella.

The butterfly hair slide flitted playfully
from side to side, its blue wings fluttering.

"Lottie! Let's put all the treasure back
into the leather bag," said Isabella. "I've
had an idea!"

"Really? What is it?" Lottie stuffed the
gold statue, the coins and the monkey
mask into the bag, just as Amina and
Rosalind ran back to them.

"Wow!" gasped Rosalind. "The hair slide is flying!"

"The polish I brought in the rucksack made it do that," said Lottie.

"All we need to do now is fasten the hair slide to the bag," said Isabella. "And then maybe it will carry the whole bag away."

"That is a really strange plan," said Rosalind. "I like it! But have we got any string to tie it on with?"

"Here! Use my hair bobble." Amina took a hairband out of her pocket and handed it over.

Isabella gently took hold of the flying butterfly hair slide and looped the hairband round it. Then she twisted the other end round one of the bag's red beads, so that the butterfly still had space to flap its wings. The jewelled creature struggled for a moment, then it flew upwards, lifting the whole bag with it.

"It's magical!" gasped Amina.

The bag soared upwards through the leaves.

"It's working!" Isabella bit her lip. "I wish it would fly right over to the baby monkey, then he could catch a ride . . ."

But just then, a furry brown shape came swinging through the branches. Petro had seen Isabella fasten the butterfly hair slide to the bag. His little eyes gleamed and he sprang forward, catching hold of the bag and clinging on.

"No, Petro!" called Isabella.

But it was too late.

The bag with the gold, pulled by the sapphire butterfly, went floating upwards. Petro dangled underneath it with a very surprised look on his furry face. It looked like he was holding on to a balloon. Up and up went the bag. It left the island behind and went flying across the river.

The treasure hunters were talking among themselves and looking over at the island. None of them had spotted the flying bag of treasure.

"Fly across to the baby monkey!" Isabella called softly, and the butterfly changed direction, heading towards the right tree as if it could understand her.

"I think it heard you," said Rosalind. "Try it again!"

"Fly up a bit more! Fly right past the baby monkey!" called the princesses, more loudly this time.

Mr Madelo glared across at them, as if he wondered what they were yelling about.

The man swung his axe against the tree again. Bang! The tree shuddered. The baby monkey climbed to the tip of the highest branch, as if he was trying to get away from the horrible noise.

"Why doesn't he jump across to the next tree?" asked Amina worriedly.

"He doesn't know what to do without his mother," said Isabella, tears springing to her eyes.

"Fly closer, butterfly hair slide!" shouted Lottie.

"Go over to the little monkey," called Rosalind, and the blue butterfly flew higher and higher.

The tree creaked even louder and began to tip sideways. The princesses held their breath, their eyes fixed on the little baby monkey. But just as the tree started to fall, the bag of treasure sailed right overhead with Petro chattering happily underneath it.

"Petro!" cried Isabella. "Catch the baby monkey!"

Petro called urgently to the baby, who held out one tiny arm. Isabella was scared that the treasure bag would sail away too fast, but the baby monkey managed to jump from his branch and cling on to Petro's back. The two monkeys floated away together above the treetops, underneath the bag of gold.

The men yelled furiously as they saw the precious gold sailing away into the sky.

"Fly away to the palace, blue butterfly!" Isabella called to the butterfly with the sapphire wings. "Fly to the palace right now!"

"I hope it gets there before the magic wears off!" said Lottie, looking at the writing on the pot of polish. "It says here it doesn't last for very long."

"Oh, no!" cried Isabella. "Then Petro and the baby monkey would fall out of the sky with the bag of gold. They could be really hurt!"

## Chapter Eleven

# The Flying Treasure

Isabella watched anxiously as the
sapphire butterfly lifted the bag of gold
away over the treetops. The baby monkey
held on tight to Petro, looking much
happier than before.

The treasure hunters ran after the gold,
shouting and arguing.

"We have to get off this island and
follow them!" cried Rosalind.

"Come on, then," said Isabella,
hurriedly stuffing the pot of polish back

into the rucksack. "I know a shortcut back to the palace that the men won't know."

It took a little while to find a fallen branch long enough and straight enough to make a new bridge over the river. Amina swung across the water and helped them put the new branch in place. Then they crossed over as fast as they could. Ahead of them, they could hear the yells of the treasure hunters.

"We have to get there first!" Isabella plunged through the trees with her brown curls bouncing on her shoulders.

They rushed back to the Palace of Belatina and ran through the tall gates just as Petro, the baby monkey and the treasure bag sailed overhead. The bag was definitely lower now.

"We'll catch you, Petro!" called Isabella, running after him.

"How did you get here before us?" growled Mr Madelo, as the treasure hunters arrived at the palace gates, red-faced from running. "That gold is ours! You girls have no right to take it."

"I thought you said you were going to give half of it to my dad?" said Isabella.

"Oh, we were never really going to give any to him," replied one man, before the others shushed him.

The blue butterfly was dipping lower now, bringing the bag of gold with it. It flew across the palace gardens, only just missing the top of a statue. The princesses ran along behind it, their arms outstretched. The treasure hunters thundered after them.

"Get the gold!" yelled Mr Madelo.

"Don't worry, little monkey!" cried Isabella. "I'll catch you if you fall, but please hang on if you can!"

The leather bag floated down towards the white palace. Isabella ran up the palace steps so fast that she nearly tripped over. She steadied herself. She had to catch the baby monkey safely. The sapphire butterfly gave one last flap of its blue wings and turned into a normal hair slide once more.

Fixing her eyes on the little monkey, Isabella reached up for him just as the bag fell towards the ground. She caught him and hugged him tight. He looked up at her with big black eyes.

"That was an awesome catch, Isabella!" said Lottie.

Petro leapt down from the bag and danced around as if he'd enjoyed flying through the air enormously. The bag of gold fell on to the steps with a clunk just as the king came to the front door. The butterfly slide broke loose from the hairband and landed beside it.

"What is all this noise?" said the king sternly. "Good gracious, Isabella! Is that you? What funny green clothes you're wearing!"

"Yes, it's me, Dad!" Isabella kissed the little monkey on his head. His fur was so soft and warm. He really was the cutest baby monkey she'd ever seen!

"Hey! Where's our treasure?" grumbled one of the men, as they stumbled up the path behind the princesses. "How did they get that bag to fly?"

"Did someone say treasure?" The king's eyes lit up. "Is this the famous lost gold?" He hurried to open the bag and pulled out a handful of gold coins. "This is excellent! But who found it all?" He looked from the princesses in their ninja outfits to the treasure hunters.

"We found the treasure!" said Isabella.

"They stole it from us, Your Majesty!" said Mr Madelo angrily, and the other men murmured in agreement. "It was supposed to be ours . . . I mean, we were finding it for you!" He swept a low bow.

Lottie stepped forward. "We heard these men say that they didn't really know where the gold was at all and that they would just chop down trees until they found it. So we had to find the treasure first and stop them."

"It's true, Dad!" said Isabella. "This little monkey nearly fell out of a tree that they were chopping down. Then Petro saved him!" She showed him the tiny monkey, who was holding on to her thumb with one little hand.

King Victor looked from the gold coins to the baby monkey and his face went very red. "You princesses have been kind and caring. I'm sad to say that I've been thinking about the lost gold so much that I forgot what's really important."

"Er, Your Majesty?" said Mr Madelo. "I can see you're busy, so we'll just take our half of the gold and go." He started to reach for the bag of treasure but one of the palace guards stopped him.

"I am more disappointed with myself than with you, Mr Madelo," the king told him. "After all, I was the one that gave you permission to chop down the trees. But now I realise that I was wrong."

Mr Madelo groaned. "But, King Victor . . ."

"This gold," the king went on, "will be going into a museum so that everyone can learn more about the ancient people who hid it. And if you need to earn some money, you can come back first thing tomorrow to help me clear up the fallen trees and plant new ones in their places."

"Yes, Your Majesty!" The men bowed and trudged away to the palace gates, their shoulders drooping.

The princesses grinned at each other in delight.

"Can we plant some new trees in the forest, too?" asked Rosalind, her blue eyes sparkling.

"Yes, we would really love to help," added Amina.

"That's a marvellous idea. I am very pleased that you care about wildlife so much." King Victor stroked the baby monkey's head and smiled. "Now, why don't you go and ask Josefina for some fruit? This monkey looks hungry to me!" He gave the monkey one last pat before he went inside.

Isabella stooped to pick up the butterfly hair slide. Then two strong-looking palace guards came down the steps to carry away the gold.

"We'd better put this hair slide back in my mum's jewellery box straightaway," said Isabella, wiping the last smear of polish off its sapphire wings. "If I tried to tell my mum how it flew through the air, I don't think she would ever believe me!"

## Chapter Twelve

# The Baby
# Monkey

The princesses took Petro and the baby
monkey up to Isabella's bedroom and
fetched lots of oranges, bananas and
pineapple for them to eat.

"Tomorrow morning when the sun
comes up, we must take this baby back
to the rainforest and help him find his
family again," said Isabella.

The other princesses nodded.

There was a knock at the door and
Queen Neva came in. "Princesses!" she

said, looking shocked. "The king said you were dressed very oddly and now I see what he meant. What are those strange clothes you're wearing?"

Isabella thought quickly; she couldn't tell her mum about the Rescue Princesses. No one else must ever know about that. So what could she say? Lottie gave her a warning look.

Suddenly Isabella knew exactly what to say. She picked up her camera from her dressing table. "Well, you see, in these dark green clothes we blend in with the leaves in the forest and that means that we don't startle the animals. Maybe I'll be able to take a picture of the Blue Morpho butterfly now that I've got these clothes to wear."

The queen seemed to accept the explanation. "Make sure you get changed now and give your hair a really good brush," she said. "The banquet will be ready in ten minutes." She smiled before closing the door behind her.

Lottie picked up another piece of orange for the baby monkey. "It's amazing to think that the clues to finding the lost gold were in your dad's study all this time, Isabella," she said.

Rosalind stood up very suddenly, her blue eyes wide. "Do you think the lost *Book of Ninja* is in there, too, Isabella?"

Isabella shook her head. "I don't think so. I'm sure I would have seen it."

Rosalind's face fell.

"We have a really huge library in our palace in Kamala," said Amina. "And we have a special section which tells you where important books from around the world are kept."

"Can you imagine how much we could learn from the *Book of Ninja*?" said

Rosalind dreamily. "It tells you how to do every single ninja move! You *will* look for it in your library in Kamala, won't you, Amina?"

"I'll have a really good look when I get back home," Amina promised her.

There was the sound of dishes clattering downstairs and Isabella suddenly remembered the banquet. "We'd better get dressed quickly!" she said.

The others rushed back to their own rooms. Isabella brushed her long brown curls and put on her favourite dress, a red one with wavy edges. Then she added her swirly gold tiara and a yellow topaz necklace to match her special ring.

Carefully, she picked up the baby monkey and he seemed happy to snuggle into her arms. Then she went to meet the other princesses in the corridor, with Petro scampering behind her.

Amina was already waiting at the top of the stairs. Her stomach made a rumbling sound. She clutched it and giggled. "I'm glad it's dinner time," she said. "I'm really hungry." She swept her long black hair over her shoulders and the emerald ring on her finger sparkled. Her long turquoise dress swept down to the floor and a silver crown was perched on her head.

"Me too!" said Rosalind. "I hope there's something nice to eat!" She smoothed away the creases in her dark blue dress. On top of her blonde hair, she wore a tiara with lots of tiny blue jewels that matched her sapphire ring.

Lottie came out of her room last, wearing a crimson dress. A ruby tiara rested on her tight red curls, matching her ruby ring. "That was a really exciting day." She grinned. "I think we're getting better and better at animal rescues!"

"I love being a Rescue Princess! I'm starting to think that princesses can do anything," said Amina happily. "Oh, wait! What's that funny noise?"

Petro leapt up on to the stair rail right next to Amina. He fixed his big black eyes on her and chattered earnestly.

Isabella laughed. "I think Petro wants you to remember it wasn't just princesses that helped this time." She smiled at him. "You're quite right, Petro! You're not a Rescue Princess, but you were really brave today!"

"Sorry, Petro, I didn't mean to leave you out!" Amina kissed the top of his furry head.

Petro leapt across to Amina's shoulder and nuzzled her ear, making them all laugh.

"I'm so happy that we helped to

keep the rainforest safe," said Isabella, hugging the baby monkey tightly. "I wonder what our next adventure will be!"

Can't wait for
The Rescue Princesses's next
daring animal adventure?

The Shimmering Stone

Turn the page for
a sneaky peek!

## Chapter One

# The Royal Wedding

Princess Amina tiptoed into the palace courtyard and peered out from behind a pillar, clutching her binoculars in one hand. Her long black hair hung loosely over her turquoise dress. She wore a bracelet with a golden-brown stone that shimmered as she moved.

She looked around carefully. Rows of tables were laid out in the centre of the courtyard, ready for the banquet tonight. There was nobody here. If she was quick,

maybe she could reach the garden
without being seen. She cast one last look
around before darting out of her hiding
place and running across the courtyard.
She'd nearly reached the other side when
she ran straight into her cousin, Princess
Rani, and tumbled to the ground.

Rani, who was much older and taller,
helped her up. "Hey!" she said, laughing.
"What's the hurry? Is there a wild animal
chasing you?"

"Oh, sorry, Rani! I didn't see you!"
gasped Amina.

"Don't worry, I'm all right!" said Rani.
"But why are you in such a rush?"

"I was looking out of the bedroom
window with my binoculars and I'm
sure I saw a tiger outside the palace
wall!" explained Amina. "It was huge
and orange, and it was walking through
the long grass beside the river. I was just

going to the wall to get a closer look." She held out her binoculars. "Oh no!" She stopped and looked at them more closely.

"What's wrong?" asked Rani.

"One of the lenses is broken. I must have knocked it against the ground when I fell over." She showed her cousin the crack in the glass on one side of the binoculars. Her heart sank. She used her binoculars nearly every day. They were so handy for seeing all the Kamalan wildlife.

"What a shame!" said Rani sympathetically. "I know how much you love them. Come and show me the tiger – we can close one eye and look through the side that isn't broken."

"All right, then," Amina turned towards the archway that led out to the garden.

"Rani! Amina! Where are you? I need you!" A loud voice rang out from inside.

Amina froze. Her aunt, Queen Keshi, had been hurrying around the palace all morning. With the royal visitors due to arrive that day there was lots to do.

"Mum wants us," said Rani. "We'll have to look for your tiger later."

"But he might have gone by then!" Amina looked longingly at the archway. If only she could get through before her aunt came along. She wanted to see the tiger so much!

"You go, then!" said Rani. "Mum probably wants me to try on my wedding dress for the hundredth time! You should go and have some fun."

Amina grinned. Even though Rani was so much older, she was a perfect cousin – kind and funny! Amina was so happy that she was going to be her bridesmaid tomorrow.

"There you are!" Queen Keshi climbed

down the steps to the courtyard, wearing a purple sari dress and a gold crown. "Rani, you must try on your wedding dress one more time. Amina, I have some jobs for you to do. The royal guests are already starting to arrive and I am determined that this shall be the best wedding ever held in the Kingdom of Kamala!"

"But Aunt!" began Amina. "Could I go out into the garden first because—"

Queen Keshi waved her hands. "Amina! There isn't much time! We must get the table decorations right and then we have to check that the guests' rooms are ready."

Amina's shoulders drooped. She wished she could go and see the tiger first. She'd seen deer and monkeys near the palace before, but never a tiger.

Rani noticed her disappointed face.

"Maybe Amina could pick some flowers from the garden to decorate the tables?" she said. "Perhaps some of those pink and white lilies."

Amina perked up. If she was picking flowers in the garden, then she could sneak a look over the wall with her binoculars at the same time!